Books for Oliver

BY **Jim Larkin and Lee Elliott Rambo**

ILLUSTRATIONS BY **Dan Brown**

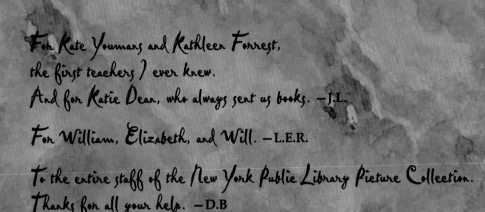

For Kate Youmans and Kathleen Forrest,
the first teachers I ever knew.
And for Katie Dean, who always sent us books. —J.L.

For William, Elizabeth, and Will. —L.E.R.

To the entire staff of the New York Public Library Picture Collection.
Thanks for all your help. —D.B

Text copyright ©2007 by Jim Larkin and Lee Elliott Rambo
Illustrations copyright ©2007 by Dan Brown
under exclusive license to Mondo Publishing

MONDO Publishing
980 Avenue of the Americas
New York, NY 10018
Visit our website at www.mondopub.com

Printed in China
09 10 11 12   9 8 7 6 5 4 3

ISBN 1-59336-336-2

Design by E. Friedman
Library of Congress Cataloging-in-Publication Data

Larkin, Jim, 1965-
  Books for Oliver / written by Jim Larkin and Lee Elliott Rambo ;
illustrated by Dan Brown.
     p. cm.
  Summary: Living in the highlands of Kenya, Oliver is happy
to be going to school, but he and his parents worry about how
they will afford to buy his textbooks.
  ISBN 1-59336-336-2 (hardcover) — ISBN 1-59336-337-0 (pbk.)
  [1. Schools--Fiction. 2. Kenya--Fiction.] I. Rambo, Lee Elliot,
1965- II. Brown, Dan, 1949- ill. III. Title.
PZ7.L323155Boo 2006
[Fic]--dc22
2005007631

Oliver Kipmutai woke to the sweet smell of wood smoke coming through the window of the one-room house he shared with his mother and father. *Breakfast time!* he thought as he wiped the sleep out of his eyes. *And a new school day!* He got up, walked to the window, and looked across the dirt yard toward the cooking fire. He could hear his mother humming as she prepared breakfast. The morning sun was warming the green grass on the hillside, and a steady breeze danced through the broad leaves of the nearby banana trees.

Oliver lived on his family's farm in Mugango, a small village in the Kenya Highlands. From the window he could see the big field out front where his family raised corn and tea. On the other side, near the road, was a smaller field, where their milk cow would spend the day happily grazing. And in a garden next to the house, the family raised an array of vegetables. Oliver and his parents ate some of the food they grew on their farm, and sold the rest at the market in the nearby village. Behind the house, tall grasses grew that Oliver's mother wove into baskets. They sold the baskets at the market, too.

Inside the mud house it was still cool. Oliver watched as Baba, his father, led their cow out to the pasture. After making sure the cow was secure, he returned to the house for breakfast. Oliver waited in the doorway as his father approached.

4

"Good morning!" his father smiled, wrapping Oliver in his strong arms. "Get dressed and come have some breakfast. You don't want to be late for school." Oliver would start his third week of school that morning. He felt more grown up and far more important than he had last year.

Oliver dressed in his school uniform and went out to eat breakfast with his parents. The cooking fire grew gradually smaller as Oliver hungrily ate his share of the cornmeal porridge from the family's big bowl.

"Do you want more ugali?" his mother asked, stirring the pot with a large wooden spoon.

"Yes, please!" Oliver answered readily, watching as his mother spooned more porridge into the bowl. Even though he had ugali every morning, and sometimes for lunch and supper too, Oliver happily ate another portion.

His mother also gave him a cup of tea. Oliver enjoyed having breakfast with his family, but he was eager to get to school. He liked being with his friends. Sometimes he never wanted the school day to end.

"Mama, how long will I be a student?"

"Oh, for many years, Oliver," his mother responded. "There is so much to learn!"

6

But Oliver also enjoyed working on the farm and going to market with his father. "Baba, when can I work on the farm with you?"

"You already help me here," his father replied, "but now is the time to learn all you can in school. A sound education will make you a good farmer. One day, this farm will be yours."

Oliver swallowed another spoonful of porridge and smiled. He was proud of the beautiful farm that his father, grandfather, and even his great-grandfather had built and tended through the years. Oliver knew that he had much to learn. He would have to work hard to be ready to run the farm one day. He drank his tea. The cow mooed placidly in the field as the morning sun's rays settled warmly on her back.

When Oliver had almost finished his ugali, his father stood up. "What are you going to do about your school books, Oliver?" he inquired.

Most schools in Kenya do not have enough money to purchase textbooks, so students need to bring their own—even poor students. Most of the students Oliver knew were poor. He had been excited when his teacher, Mrs. Langat, told the class about their schoolbooks—this was the first year that he was old enough to need books of his own to use in his studies.

"Mrs. Langat said we have two weeks to get our books, Baba," Oliver reassured him.

Oliver's mother glanced over at him. "Two weeks have already passed," she pointed out. "We need to have your books this week. Have you come up with any ideas about how we're to buy them?"

8

"No," Oliver replied softly. "Aren't you going to get them for me?"

Oliver's father sighed. "We've thought about it a great deal, Oliver. To buy the things we need at home, we sell our crops and your mother's baskets. Books are important, but we can't eat books, and we don't have any extra money."

"Perhaps your teacher will give you a few more days to get your books," his mother offered hopefully.

Oliver smiled tentatively. He liked Mrs. Langat and knew that she liked him, too. He thought that maybe she would be able to help. He would ask her right after the morning session of classes had ended.

"Well, I'm off to town to do some trading," his father announced. "And it's time for you to get to school, Oliver."

Oliver said good-bye to his mother and waited for his father. Together they walked down the path, past rows of corn and tea, until they reached the road.

"Good-bye!" said Oliver cheerfully.

"Good-bye!" his father echoed as he followed the road toward the village.

10

Oliver raced over to the cow grazing in the small pasture and patted her nose affectionately. He looked back toward his father as a thought occurred to him. "What are you going to trade at the market?" Oliver shouted, but his father had already journeyed too far down the road to hear him. The cow blinked her large, soft eyes at Oliver as he set off down the same road in the opposite direction.

As he walked past other farms and grass-roofed homes, Oliver felt lucky to live in the Kenya Highlands. The Nygores River flowed nearby, and the cool, damp ground felt good under his bare feet. All around him the countryside was green, lush, and full of life. He took a deep breath and smelled the sweet plumeria blossoms mixed with the scent of smoke from nearby breakfast fires. Neighbors doing their morning chores called out "Jambo!" and waved in greeting to Oliver as he walked by. He, too, shouted "Jambo!" as he waved back.

Oliver took his usual shortcut through a neighbor's cornfield, and a few minutes later he arrived at school. His friends Apili, James, and Nasambu were rolling tires in the grassy fields that surrounded the school. Oliver joined in, running and laughing in the morning breeze. But after a few short minutes, the principal pulled the long rope that rang the school bell. It was time for classes to begin. Oliver and his friends brushed themselves off and went to join their classmates for morning lessons.

"Come earlier tomorrow, Oliver," Apili reminded him. "We'll have more time to play!"

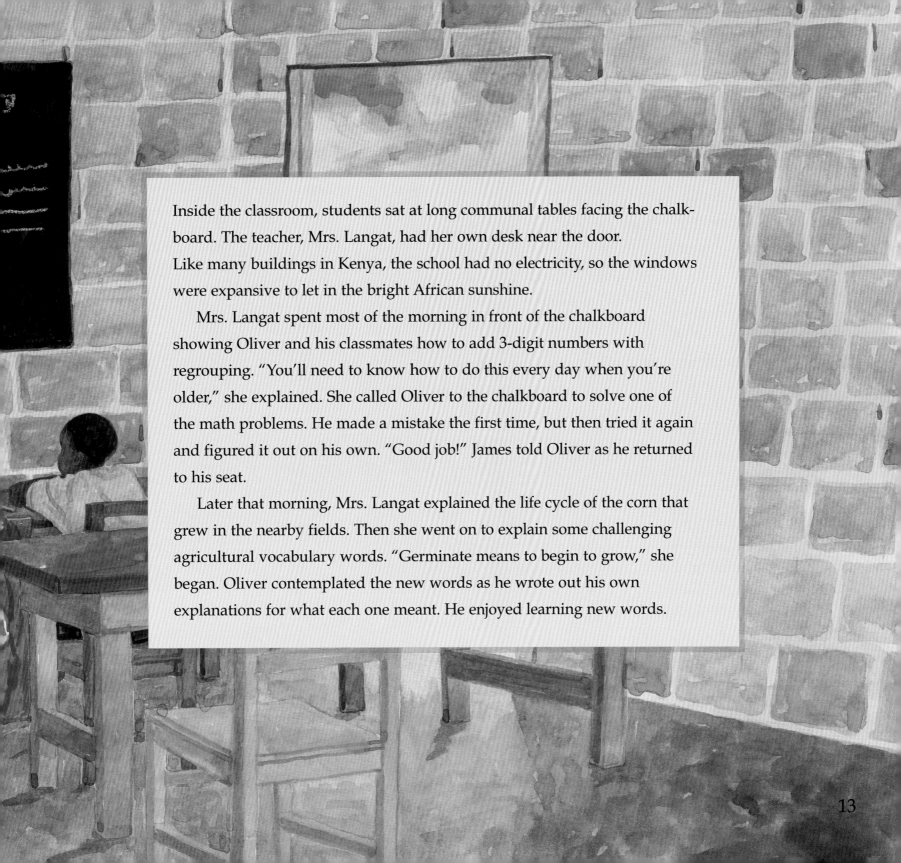

Inside the classroom, students sat at long communal tables facing the chalkboard. The teacher, Mrs. Langat, had her own desk near the door.
Like many buildings in Kenya, the school had no electricity, so the windows were expansive to let in the bright African sunshine.

Mrs. Langat spent most of the morning in front of the chalkboard showing Oliver and his classmates how to add 3-digit numbers with regrouping. "You'll need to know how to do this every day when you're older," she explained. She called Oliver to the chalkboard to solve one of the math problems. He made a mistake the first time, but then tried it again and figured it out on his own. "Good job!" James told Oliver as he returned to his seat.

Later that morning, Mrs. Langat explained the life cycle of the corn that grew in the nearby fields. Then she went on to explain some challenging agricultural vocabulary words. "Germinate means to begin to grow," she began. Oliver contemplated the new words as he wrote out his own explanations for what each one meant. He enjoyed learning new words.

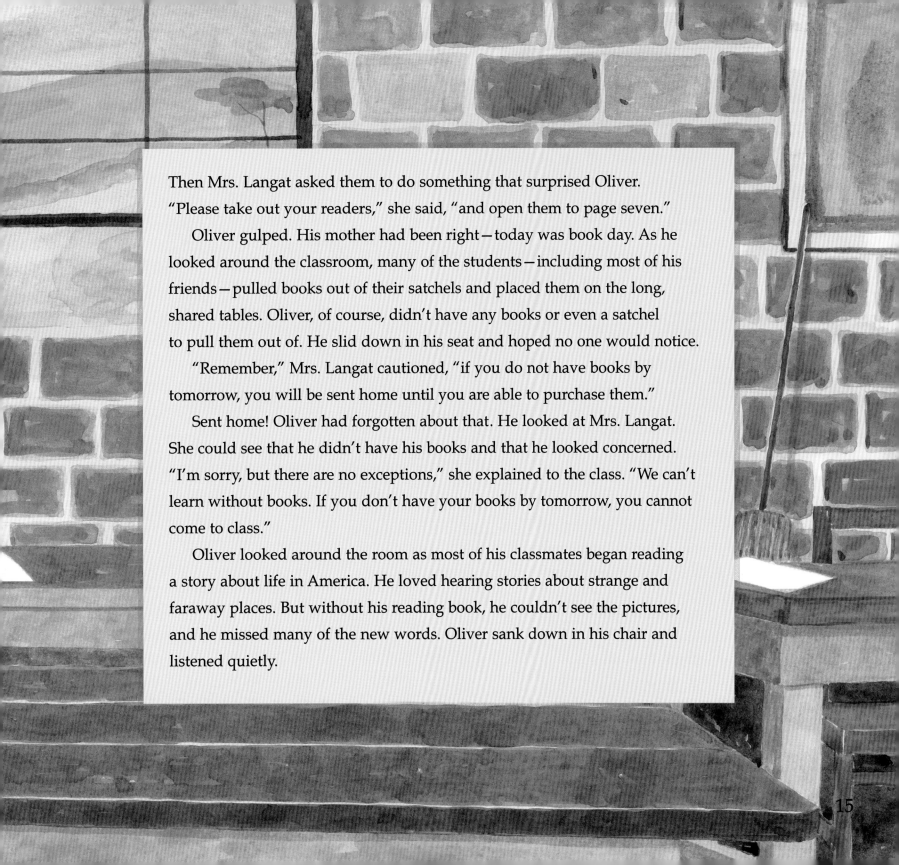

Then Mrs. Langat asked them to do something that surprised Oliver. "Please take out your readers," she said, "and open them to page seven."

Oliver gulped. His mother had been right—today was book day. As he looked around the classroom, many of the students—including most of his friends—pulled books out of their satchels and placed them on the long, shared tables. Oliver, of course, didn't have any books or even a satchel to pull them out of. He slid down in his seat and hoped no one would notice.

"Remember," Mrs. Langat cautioned, "if you do not have books by tomorrow, you will be sent home until you are able to purchase them."

Sent home! Oliver had forgotten about that. He looked at Mrs. Langat. She could see that he didn't have his books and that he looked concerned. "I'm sorry, but there are no exceptions," she explained to the class. "We can't learn without books. If you don't have your books by tomorrow, you cannot come to class."

Oliver looked around the room as most of his classmates began reading a story about life in America. He loved hearing stories about strange and faraway places. But without his reading book, he couldn't see the pictures, and he missed many of the new words. Oliver sank down in his chair and listened quietly.

15

At noon, the students left school and headed to their respective homes for lunch. Oliver walked down the hill with Mrs. Langat, hoping to speak to her about his books. As Oliver's schoolmates hurried past, he noticed Mr. Chelule, the maintenance worker, clearing overgrown grasses beside the school with a machete. Remembering his task, Oliver turned back to Mrs. Langat. "If I don't have my school books tomorrow," he asked, "would you please give me a few more days?" The bright sunshine made him squint as he looked up into her eyes.

Mrs. Langat was always pleasant to Oliver. She smiled at him as she stopped to speak. "Oliver, you've already had two weeks. Without your books, learning will be difficult."

"But you'll teach me," Oliver offered hopefully.

"Books help you to teach yourself," she explained. "Even a teacher can't show you everything there is to learn. Without your books, you would only hear part of the stories—you couldn't see how words are spelled. You wouldn't have examples of how to do the math. And it wouldn't be fair to the students who did bring in their books."

Oliver dug his toe into the dirt as he thought this over.

"No, the rule is that if you don't have your books, then you must be sent home," she said. "I like having you in class very much, but the rules must be the same for everyone. I'm sorry, Oliver."

17

At the bottom of the hill, Oliver said good-bye and turned onto the path that led to his house. A thought suddenly occurred to him. If his parents didn't have the money to buy books, maybe he could earn it. Oliver passed his neighbor's house and wondered if Mr. Kibit would pay him to help milk his cows. But then Oliver saw Mr. Kibit's three strong sons out in the field and realized that Mr. Kibit certainly wouldn't need any extra help.

Oliver walked on slowly while he considered his dilemma, absentmindedly running his fingers through the tall grass along the river path. He saw the gristmill up ahead by the water's edge, and stopped. Maybe he could work for Mr. Mutende at the mill, grinding corn into meal. But then he remembered that the mill operated only during the daylight hours when he needed to be in school. That wouldn't work either.

As Oliver got closer to home, he could hear the cow mooing in the field. A few steps later, he rounded the bend and spotted her chewing on tufts of sweet grass. "Moo!" Oliver called in greeting. The cow blinked at him, then lowered her head to collect another mouthful.

Oliver walked deliberately down the path toward the yard. His mother was kneeling over the fire, preparing lunch. She looked up when she heard him approach. "Jambo, Oliver!" she called out with a smile.

She could see that he was deep in thought about something. "What's wrong?" she asked.

Oliver told his mother what had happened at school. Cautiously, he asked if they had found any extra money to buy his books.

"No, we haven't, Oliver," she replied softly. She stood up and put her arm around his shoulder. "But just because a problem is difficult doesn't mean there isn't a solution." As she spoke, Oliver's father appeared from around the side of the house.

"Baba, what are you doing home? Why aren't you at the market?" Oliver questioned, surprised at his father's sudden appearance.

"I came home to eat lunch and to see my favorite son," he laughed, and threw his arm around Oliver's small shoulders.

As they ate, Baba began telling stories about his morning at the market. There had been so much corn and tea for sale that it might be difficult to sell what they'd grown. A family on the road to town told him that they were looking to buy a cow. And Mr. Towett had bought two big roosters for his farm.

Oliver thought that he would never get to ask his father about the books. Finally, Baba asked him about school, and Oliver told him everything—he didn't have his schoolbooks, time was up, and he couldn't think of a way to get them by tomorrow.

"You've been thinking hard about this, haven't you?" Baba asked. Oliver nodded silently. "Well, I've been thinking about it, too," his father continued. Oliver looked up at him with a hopeful expression. "It is a difficult situation, but you can't give up on something important just because it's difficult, right?" Baba said, echoing his wife's words as he took another sip of tea.

Oliver hoped his father had come up with a magnificent idea, but nothing more was said. They finished their lunch in silence.

Oliver left his parents finishing their noon meal and began his walk back to school. He walked right past the cow, the gristmill, and the Kibet farm without even noticing them. Oliver was thinking about books. In fact, he decided that the most difficult math problems in school were simple compared to his book problem. No matter how hard he tried, he couldn't think of a solution.

When the school bell rang to mark the end of the day, Oliver walked slowly out of the classroom. He was no closer to an answer to his problem. Apili, Nasambu, and James were already outside and wanted to look at their new books once more. They sat in a small circle on the ground and eagerly opened their satchels. Oliver stood just outside their circle, looking sadly over his friends' shoulders.

Nasambu opened her reader to a picture of an adult male lion. "This was my sister's book last year," she explained when she noticed Oliver looking forlornly at the photograph.

James opened one of the books that his mother had bought by trading some chickens. His family had a large farm. "Look at all those math problems!" he gasped, his eyes growing wide with horror.

"They're just numbers," Apili laughed. He was good with numbers. "We'll all learn it together." But with no books, how would Oliver learn anything? As he waved good-bye to his friends, he wondered if this had been his last day in school.

A little way down the path, he saw Mr. Chelule again. He was not clearing away the tall grasses in the schoolyard anymore. He had stopped to rest and have a drink of water.

"Jambo, Oliver!"

"Jambo, Mr. Chelule," Oliver replied. "Where's Mr. Mwembe?" Mr. Mwembe usually helped Mr. Chelule keep the school clean and tidy.

"He's at home today. He's not feeling well," Mr. Chelule said.

Oliver had a thought. "Do you need any help?" he asked. "I help my father often on our farm. I could help you too, but you'd have to pay me. Could you do that?"

Mr. Chelule chuckled. "Well, yes—I could use your help today. And I'll gladly pay you to help me, Oliver."

Oliver was thrilled. Here was the answer! He would have his books tomorrow after all. "Can you pay me today?" he asked.

"I don't see why not," Mr. Chelule replied with a smile.

Oliver began clearing away what Mr. Chelule had already cut. Later, Oliver used the machete to cut more of the coarse grass, and as the day began to cool down, he carried away some big rocks that Mr. Chelule had dug out of the schoolyard.

Mr. Chelule called to Oliver across the field. "That's enough for today, Oliver. You're a hard worker! Your parents must be proud of you."

Oliver smiled and waited for his reward. Mr. Chelule reached into his pocket and gave Oliver several shiny coins. "Here you are, Oliver, and thank you. You were an able assistant today. Please tell your parents hello for me."

Oliver looked down at his money as Mr. Chelule walked back to the tool shed. He had earned some money, but not nearly enough to pay for schoolbooks. At this rate, he would have to work for days and days before he would have enough. Oliver put the coins in his pocket and wiped his eyes quickly before anyone noticed his tears of frustration. Then he took a deep breath, straightened his tired shoulders, and headed down the path toward home.

As he got close to the house, Oliver listened for the sound of their cow. He didn't hear anything. When he could finally see the field, the cow was nowhere in sight. Oliver was startled. Had she wandered away? He ran into the house.

"Mama, where is the cow?" His mother was weaving a beautiful, bowl-shaped basket.

"Your father took the cow to town, to the market," she said.

"But why?" Oliver asked, confused. His father never took the cow anywhere.

"He's going to sell the cow to the family down the road. They need a cow, and with the money, Baba can buy your books," she said. Oliver couldn't believe it. The cow was important to the family.

"He would sell our cow? How will we get milk? We need the cow, don't we, Mama?" he asked.

"But you need books, Oliver," she said, taking his chin in her hand. "It will be difficult to get by without the cow, but we want you to go to school, and that is not possible without books."

His father would sell the family's only cow to buy his books! Oliver was speechless. He couldn't believe it.

"Please sweep the yard, Oliver," his mother said. "Your father will not be home until late tonight, after supper."

Oliver swept the yard, and then went out to where the cow would usually be wandering around in her grassy pasture. He chased a butterfly, waved at Mrs. Chelule on the road, and then lay down among some wildflowers and thought about getting his books. Now he would be able to read stories about other countries and other people, and he could learn how to solve long division problems. There were so many things in books that he wanted to know.

When the sun was low in the sky, almost behind the hills, it was time for supper. Oliver looked around the empty field before he went inside to eat. He would miss the cow.

Just before bedtime his mother called out, "Oliver, your father's home."

Oliver ran outside and down the path to greet his father, but when he saw Baba, he stopped. Standing there next to his father was the cow, who blinked at him as she chewed a mouthful of grass. Oliver was happy to see the cow, but he wondered if he would still get his schoolbooks. He walked to the shed with his father to bed her down. Then they sat in the doorway looking up at the night sky.

"The family I mentioned to you bought another cow just before I got there," his father said. "I'm sorry, Oliver."

"Is there another way to buy the books, Baba?" Oliver asked.

If he had another idea, Oliver's father did not tell him. It was dark now. Inside, Baba helped Oliver unroll his sleeping mat and pulled the mosquito netting over his head to keep the bugs away. Then he went back out into the warm African night. Oliver fell asleep wondering what would happen the next day.

He woke to the sound of a jangling cowbell. It was still dark outside, and Oliver was surprised that their cow was already out in the field. He rubbed his eyes and looked around the room. His parents were not there, which meant it must be morning. Oliver went to look out the small round window at the pasture. There was a cow in the field, but it wasn't their cow. It was a cow he'd never seen before! He looked closer—there were two cows!

Oliver heard his father and another man talking. When he got to the doorway, he saw Baba bringing their cow to the small patch of grass by the house. His father came inside after making sure the cow was securely tied.

"Someone else's cows are in our pasture!" Oliver said to him. "They're on our land!"

His father didn't say anything as he put his hand on Oliver's head.

"Why is our cow tied on this little bit of grass?" Oliver asked anxiously. "Why are those other cows in our pasture?"

"Oliver," his father said quietly, "that isn't our property anymore. The man who wanted another cow needed more land for his cows to graze on, so I sold him our pasture."

"You sold some of our land?" Oliver's eyes got big.

His father pointed toward the doorway. Oliver could see that there was something just outside on the ground. "But we have these now," Baba said.

Oliver walked to the doorway and looked outside. Sitting on the ground was a small stack of books tied up with twine. He looked up at his father, who was smiling. Oliver was smiling, too. His mother walked over and knelt down next to him. "They're yours," she said, handing him a scuffed but sturdy satchel. "You can put them in this."

Oliver picked up his new schoolbooks— the first books he had ever owned—and took them over to a little stump near the cow. Carefully, he untied the twine. He was still smiling as he sat down and started turning the pages. Math, spelling, stories—he had so much to learn! As Oliver began reading, the sun came up bright and strong. Its rays reached out over hills and farmlands, illuminating every corner of Oliver's world—the beginning of a new school day.